JUST ME IN THE TUB

BY GINA AND MERCER MAYER

For Lauren Atkinson

A GOLDEN BOOK • NEW YORK

Western Publishing Company, Inc., Racine, Wisconsin 53404

Library of Congress Catalog Card Number: 93-73532   ISBN: 0-307-12816-4/ISBN: 0-307-62816-7 (lib. bdg.)   A MCMXCIV

When I take a bath, there are lots
of things that I have to do.

First I start to run the water in the tub.
I like it to be nice and warm.
Sometimes it takes a little while to
get the water just right.

Then I put in the bubble stuff. I have to be careful not to pour in too much.

While the water is running, I get my towel and washcloth. I like big fluffy towels.

I get my pajamas, too.
I always look for clean ones.

Then I take off my clothes and get into the tub.

When the water is just deep enough,
I turn it off. If I let the water run too much,
it could splash on the floor.

I always wash before
I play in my bath.

I start with my face . . .

then I wash my hair . . .

and my feet . . .

and my hands.

I wash my arms and legs . . .

and even in between my toes.

I can't reach my back,
so I use a brush for that.

Then it's time to play with my toys.
If I forget something, I never bother
Mom—I just go and get it.

I can't take my stuffed animals into the tub. But I bring them into the bathroom, so they won't feel left out.

I like to play with my pirate ship in the tub. Sometimes my pirate ship is caught in a terrible storm and ends up stranded on a desert island.

I have pots and pans to play with in the tub, too. I like to make bubble cakes. But they don't taste too good.

I can make myself look like Santa Claus.

I play in the tub until my mom says, "Time to come out now!"

I knew it was time because
the water was getting cold.

When I get out of the tub,
I step on the bath mat, so I
won't splash water everywhere.

Sometimes Mom comes in
and helps me dry off.

Then I put on my nice clean pajamas.

I always remember to let
the water drain out of the tub.
But sometimes I forget
about my toys.

Then I wipe up the
floor, just in case
I splashed a little.

And I put my
dirty clothes
in the basket.

Taking a bath can be a real job.

But it always makes me
feel warm and cozy.